KU-064-697

THIS WALKER BOOK BELONGS TO:

_____

_____

_____

_____

For Oscar

First published 1994 by
Walker Books Ltd
87 Vauxhall Walk
London SE11 5HJ

This edition published 1998

2 4 6 8 10 9 7 5 3 1

© 1994 Catherine and Laurence Anholt

This book has been typeset in Bembo.

Printed in Hong Kong

British Library Cataloguing in Publication Data
A catalogue record for this book is
available from the British Library.

ISBN 0-7445-6190-6 (Hbk)
ISBN 0-7445-6069-1 (Pbk)

WHAT MAKES ME HAPPY?

Catherine and Laurence Anholt

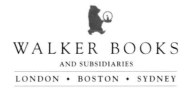

WALKER BOOKS

AND SUBSIDIARIES

LONDON • BOSTON • SYDNEY

What makes me laugh?

tickly toes

a big red nose

being rude

silly food

acting crazy

my friend Maisie

What makes me cry?

wasps that sting

a fall from a swing

wobbly wheels

head over heels

What makes me bored?

Grown-ups...

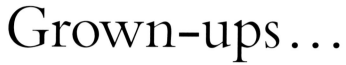

moaning   groaning   eating   meeting   walking   talking

feeding   reading   sitting   knitting   stopping   shopping

What makes me pleased?

Look how much I've grown!

I can do it on my own!

What makes us jealous?

Her!

What makes me scared?

shrieks

creaks

jaws

claws

bangs

gangs

caves

waves

What makes me sad?

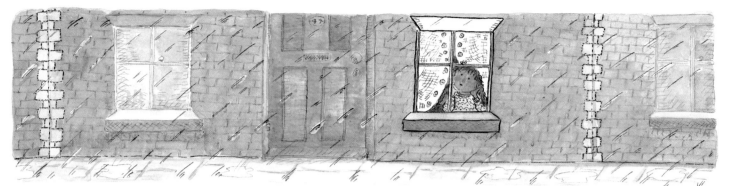

Rain, rain, every day.

No one wants to let me play.

Someone special's far away.

What makes us excited?

A roller-coaster ride

Here comes the bride!

The monster's on his way!

A party day

What makes me shy?

My first day

What makes me cross?

Days when buttons won't go straight
and I want to stay up late
and I hate what's on my plate...
Why won't anybody wait?

What makes us all happy?

making a castle

opening a parcel

singing a song

skipping along

windy weather

finding a feather and...

Being together.

MORE WALKER PAPERBACKS
For You to Enjoy
Also by Catherine and Laurence Anholt

WHAT I LIKE

"Children's likes and dislikes, as seen by six children but with a
universality which makes them appealing to all… The scant, rhyming text is elegantly fleshed out by
delicate illustrations full of tiny details." *Children's Books of the Year*

0-7445-6070-5   £4.99

KIDS

"From the absurd to the ridiculous, from the real to the imaginary, from the
nasty to the charming, this is a book which touches on the important aspects of life as
experienced by the young child." *Books for Keeps*

0-7445-6067-5   £4.99

HERE COME THE BABIES

"Over 70 warm and funny pictures of babies to amuse and entertain –
especially those with a younger brother or sister."
Practical Parenting

0-7445-6066-7   £4.99

Walker Paperbacks are available from most booksellers, or by post from B.B.C.S., P.O. Box 941, Hull, North Humberside HU1 3YQ

24 hour telephone credit card line 01482 224626

To order, send: Title, author, ISBN number and price for each book ordered, your full name and address,
cheque or postal order payable to BBCS for the total amount and allow the following for postage and packing:
UK and BFPO: £1.00 for the first book, and 50p for each additional book to a maximum of £3.50.
Overseas and Eire: £2.00 for the first book, £1.00 for the second and 50p for each additional book.
Prices and availability are subject to change without notice.